TANA HOBAN
Exactly the Opposite

Greenwillow Books
New York

The full-color photographs
were reproduced
from 35-mm. slides.
Copyright © 1990
by Tana Hoban

Greenwillow Books,
a division of William
Morrow & Company, Inc.,
1350 Avenue of the Americas,
New York, NY 10019.

Printed in Hong Kong
by South China Printing
Company (1988) Ltd.
First Edition
10 9 8 7 6 5 4 3 2

Library of Congress
Cataloging-in-Publication Data

Hoban, Tana.
Exactly the opposite /
Tana Hoban.
p.   cm.
Summary: Photographs of
familiar outdoor scenes
illustrate pairs of opposites.
ISBN 0-688-08861-9.
ISBN 0-688-08862-7 (lib. bdg.)
1. English language—
Synonyms and antonyms—
Juvenile literature.
[1. English language—
Synonyms and antonyms.]
I. Title.
PE 1591.H58   1990
428.1—dc20
89-27227   CIP   AC

This one is for Gail